AMMU

THE QUEEN WHO BROUGHT LOVE FROM HILL STATION

JAYANTH KASHYAP

Made with ♥ on the Notion Press Platform
www.notionpress.com

Dedicated to Ammu

Post writing the book "Tell Me the reason why you left" If there is one reason why I still write is the amount of love and respect I have received post publishing the book.

Hence I dedicate this book to all my readers. My dear readers, thanks for staying by my side with every publication printed.

Let's conquer the world with Love!

Contents

Foreword

Dear readers,

It is with great pleasure that I introduce you to this beautiful and touching love story penned by my closest friend. This book is a heartfelt portrayal of two individuals who fall deeply in love and navigate the complexities of their relationship with grace and determination even after the cruel play of fate.

The author has woven together a narrative which is engaging, showing the ups and downs that come with any loving relationship. The characters are relatable and endearing, and you will find yourself rooting for them throughout their journey.

This pure love story is a testament to the power of love and the importance of perseverance in the face of adversity. This story exhibits that when in love, you can cross oceans for it.

It is a story that will leave you feeling warm and fuzzy inside, and remind you of the beauty and joy that comes with finding that special someone and the sorrow which follows with love.

This book is a poignant reminder of the fragility of life and the intensity of our emotions. It is a beautifully crafted story that will resonate with readers who have experienced loss, and also those who appreciate the power of love and the strength of the human spirit.

It is a truly heartwarming and inspiring read.

I am honored to recommend this novel and congratulate the author on their ability to create such a moving and memorable work of literature.

Sincerely,

S N HITHAN GOWDA

Preface

It was love at first sight! In a world where loyalty is no more a norm, here comes a lady who demands and commands loyalty. She is fast at her speech, laughs loud, and speaks too much but there is a silence in her eyes. She loves unconditionally and cares with conditions. Friendship is no more an Instagram profile for her, it is a religion, promise given in words for her aren't mere promises, those are her commandments.

What makes an ordinary lady a special one? What makes an ordinary love story a special one? Its the amount of faith and trust the couple exhibit. This is a story based on true inspirations, this is the story of Jeev and Sweety. This is a novel on unwavering faith to be committed and wavering promise to protect!

It's the white lies and toxicity that affect any relationship, as they say, do not water the plant, for which you do not wish to grow! Yet life, love, and relationship are very complex. *This is the narration of the Blood, Sweat, and Tears! This is the story of Ammu, the queen who brought love from the hill station!*

Acknowledgements

My deepest thanks to my parents who have always supported me in all my writings, I am a very spiritual person, my deepest thanks to the almighty lord Shiva, who has been my source of strength and my protector.

My special thanks and appreciation to my set of student readers of KLE Institution who are always excited about every book I release. My love and thanks to my online readers' community which gives me unconditional love and support!

My special thanks to my friends and family members who are critical and appreciative of all my works

Prologue

During the month of September and the rainy season, it was hitting less than 12 degrees celsius in the city of Kodaikanal, it was around 26 degrees celsius in the city of Bengaluru.

Kodai is a beautiful hill station, the pure air in the Kodai must be such that it produces people with pure emotions. Bengaluru is the living city of India, It is very special because of its comforting climate, people, acceptance, and varied culture.

Kodaikanal bus station except during peak time is not filled with tourists much, but Bengaluru is filled with people, traffic, and food!

Bengaluru is the city of Startups and Kodai is the city of Love!

ONE

After the Tragedy

Phone calls rang continuously, and the manager shouted "Jeevarth, pick up the fucking phone man!" what are you doing? Jeev turned around to see the phones around him ringing, he picked up the phone and said "Hello, who is this?". It's me Swee..., oops sorry it's me Sweety Shetty from Kodaikanal. Jeev said, "Ok what do you need?". Sweety replied " I am joining the job tomorrow, can I know the exact address please?

Jeev cut the call! "Nonsense". People join the job without knowing the address. Jeev after cutting the call said, "Oh shit! Why am I exhibiting my anger on this lady?".

Jeev had undergone a tragedy in his life, Jeev's 4-year-old relationship had left him, and he was shattered to the core, adding to Jeev's wound was his office, which wanted him to work 24x7!

Jeev was an assistant software engineer in a startup, just like any other middle-class dream, he dreamt of making his life a big one by converting this startup into an unicorn company, yet something bothered him always.

Jeev's girl, sorry ex, had called Jeev a year back, she asked him if Jeev wanted to meet the boy that she is going to marry! Listening to this, Jeev cut the phone and thus Jeev's love story ended with his ex cheating in the relationship. Post the relationship Jeev had become silent, he hardly believed in the concept of falling in love. He barely kept his personal life to himself.

Jeev had spent his money, effort, emotions, career, job, and course he opted, everything for his ex, now he sat on the table devastated, he sometimes sat in the public park alone and cried loud, watchman on duty sometimes consoled him. Moving on is definitely simple is it not?

He always envied chubby girls and consciously avoided confronting them!. He was averse to girls, now more to chubby ones. Probably post-traumatic stress disorder caused by the chubby ex! Jeev was more or less an intelligent man, he ate alone and had minimum conversation with family and maximum conversation with strangers. He did not care much about money, finance, and future savings, he helped anyone who came to him. He slept late and woke up early, and felt empty.

One evening in the office the manager asked him to resign from the job, not because he was not working but because Jeev was overworking.

Jeev had lost his smile while working on the job. It was quite depressing for people to understand Jeev as he had everything but no happiness, he looked deeply empty. Nothing could actually touch or move him. His friend Gudeesh then commented on Jeev " Only a goddess from heaven can come to improve your mental health".

Yet Jeev was the kindest man one can think of, his kindness could literally kill people. Jeev donated around 20 percent of his salary to the needy ones in his neighborhood. He never tipped anything less than rupees 50 to a small hotel waiter. He ate food from a local side street vendor and never displayed arrogance. There were multiple layers to his personality. It was indeed very hard to judge him as a person. Everyone including the junior in the office, until the peons loved, respected, and cared for Jeev. As his name, he was the jeev for most of his colleagues. Jeev was a spiritual man and always preached dharma and altruism as a way one should lead their life.

TWO

THE QUEEN FROM HILL STATION!

Sweety Shetty! Chubby little damsel in distress from Kodaikanal, who had just completed her engineering called the startup to ask the address of the company she wanted to join. To her surprise, the person speaking from the other side was rude and cut the call abruptly. She was almost in tears, in a few minutes she had her bus leaving from Kodaikanal to Bengaluru. In a few minutes time, she had to rush and hop on the bus.

Her mom shouted, "Paapa what is this?" I can't send you alone like this, saying this both her amma and appa joined her to drop her to the job. On the way, they decided that they would also stay alongside their cute little princess since the tragedy that had happened earlier in their home made them so much more attached to sweety. What was the tragedy?

Sweety was not a normal girl, it was very hard to understand her, In this fake world, she was entirely the most genuine one, her love, her arrogance, her anger everything was in its purest form. It could be described as a once-in-a-lifetime you could come across such a genuine personality.

She took her bag baggage and carried tons of love to be given, to the city Bengaluru. She alongside her parents started the journey. The journey that could move mountains of love! The journey of the

Queen who brought love from hill station!

THREE

PRAKAASH

Sweety dropped at Bengaluru, her eyes filled with tears upon seeing the city, as soon as she landed in the city, she heard the song in th background '*Happy agide, happy agide*,' which means feeling happy in *Kannada*. With her wide-open smile and curly hair, she carried her luggage and said " Anna shall we go to Kashinagar" The auto driver agreed. Thus started her journey to the city. She saw the place, she was the queen from the hill station, for her seeing busy roads, vehicles, fast-moving people was all a new phenomenon.

Prakaash is Sweety's brother, wherever Sweety goes he followed her, this time too he was with Sweety. Prakash was a bike enthusiast, he loved being rowdy in their colony, he drove so fast that even death was afraid of him. The only problem with Prakaash was that he never was traveling or being with Sweety after she left for Bengaluru. He always stood far, so far that Sweety could sense that he is near but she could never see him or meet him. Why is this prakash so mysterious?

Prakash fought with his parents multiple times because he wanted to be so independent, his contacts were rowdy sheeters and other elements, which their parents never did appreciate for. There were multiple instances where he would leave the home and disappear for days. There was even a time when he attempted suicide, that literally made him go away from the parents. But his father always understood him, and ensured that Prakaash always got the love, care that he needed.

But Sweety and Prakaash's parents were gem of a people, they never complained or hurt the feelings of their children. The bonding of both the parents and their children was so strong that only a divine intervention could separate them. Neither Sweety nor their parents knew that Prakash was staying in Bengaluru.

Sweety and her parents came and made room in a local relative home. They slept happily. The next morning Sweety had to run to her first job, with loads of tension and excitement, she slept with her blanket on and her chubby cheek smiling.

But something was not right in the entire process, something was going fundamentally wrong?

FOUR

KING MEETS HIS PRINCESS

It was 9: 30 AM in the morning, Jeev had just started to train a group of trainees who had joined in the past week, Jeev was a master of communication, body language, and soft skills, he was an expert in coding. He believed that more than everything, dedication and giving 201 percent, i.e. more than what is required to the job should be given to be successful as a person! *He believed in giving more than 201 percent but the poor fellow forgot that givers are drained one day and givers must also be given.*

Sweety walked into the office with her white bag and baby kitten smile, she was welcomed by her trainee batchmates, and she felt jolly jolly after meeting a lot of people. She loved chatting, gossiping, and being among people., so much so that her entire school, college, and engineering batchmates were in still in touch with her. Sweety sat at her place and was given instruction by a voice behind, the voice said " I will distribute all of you a small verbal test to check your intelligence and interest levels in the job, please fill it out as soon as possible". Saying that the voice also commented, "Whose hairs are these so long!". She turned and saw the voice but the man with that voice walked away, she started to fill in the details of the test paper. The voice came again and it was time for her to submit the paper, she said " Sir, the paper, and she saw, and he smiled, it was

Jeev who smiled!

In all that land had never been, his smile was contagious, Sweety saw Jeev, the smile that was so genuine but the eyes spoke a million words. Jeev's eye was half teared always, they say when a person smiles, look in his eyes, you could see a million emotions! Here is a man whose eyes mesmerized Sweety!

"Madam, are you a new joiner?" asked Jeev. Sweety was silent! Jeev repeated "Madam?" Sweety had seen hundred of friends, and spoken to thousands, which never disturbed her so much. They say love at first sight, this was not love at first sight, this was an experience she underwent, she had a sudden jerk of heart-stopping, and Sweety shivered for a moment. She literally saw a man who could smile, be genuine and yet hide his emotions in his eyes, his silence bothered her. His eyes spoke and sweety fell, the queen from hill station fell in love with a man of multiple emotions, this wasn't attraction or infatuation, this was the love that the queen kept all her life to be given to this man!

The ship of love always travels assuming that it could sink anytime!

Jeev said, "Your name please?". "Sweety..Sweety Shetty". "Unique name indeed". Jeev made her feel comfortable, where are you from " Kodai..Kodaikanal", she said. "Madam then you must take me one day to Kodai, pinky promise will you". She said, "Sirr...I Will, pinky promise".

The conversation ended with Jeev leaving the workstation.

Falling in love is temporary, forgetting is forever!

Sweety never imagined that on the first day of her job, she would meet a person who could have such an impact on her. She consoled herself and spoke to her trainees and her senior trainees about the job and her senior Jeev. The only thing everyone said about Jeev was that he was a gem of a person, and who could literally move mountains to help people, some even confessed that they love Jeev so much that it is because of him that people stay in the organization still,

Sweety was touched to hear stories about Jeev. She wanted to hear more about him. It was 5 PM. She was trained by a group of senior trainees in coding. and she left, just before she left, she went in search of Jeev to tell him thanks for the induction and for making her feel at home on the first day of her job. She came in search of a job, and a better future, here she stood searching for him.

But Jeev had Left!

FIVE

A Happy New Year

The second day of Sweety's office was the eve of New Year. Sweety hadn't slept the whole night thinking about Jeev. She spoke about Jeev so much with her parents, that at one point in time, it secretly scared her parents too. She got up early and ran to her office, new to the city and language but it wasn't difficult at all for her to mingle with her office mates.

Jeev logged on time. Sweety waiting at her cabin to see Jeev, Jeev hardly smiled but smiled back at people who smiled and waved at people who wished him good morning. Jeev saw Sweety with a big smile and her eyes wanting to express something. Jeev " Sweety madam, would you like to say something?" She stood silent! Jeev continued "Sweety could you finish this coding assignment and show me if there are any bugs found". Sweety said "Okay" Jeev left

It was late in the evening, and Sweety wasn't ready to stop staring at Jeev or his training or his body language, with every sight she looked she was falling deeper in love with Jeev. At the end of the evening, before logging out, Sweety wished Jeev "Sir, wish you a happy new year". Jeev who wore a helmet, couldn't hear her properly, he said "Bye madam take care!".

The disappointed Sweety went home back seeking an answer to console herself. There popped up a whats-app notification, "You have been added to the WhatsApp group *'Jeev's Trainees'*. Sweety danced with joy, she opened the group, found Jeev's whats app number, and saved it with a heart symbol. She didn't know how to save his name in the beginning.

It was midnight 12 AM and a happy new year, Sweety who was not fast asleep, took out her phone, gathered all her courage, and texted Jeev " Sir, wish you a happy new year, may this year bring happiness, prosperity and bring back all your joy and happiness!" and she sent. She immediately switched off her phone with fear and slept.

The next morning, Sweety woke up to check the WhatsApp message, and there she found a reply from Jeev "Thank you so much madam. God bless you!". It made her new year the happiest new year. Jeev here became quite suspicious of the new joiner's message, he sensed something wasn't right.

Something was wrong, and something was off! What was it?

SIX

COMMITTED TO DEATH

It was a bright little day at the office, Sweety had just walked into and Jeev called her into his cabin to speak to her, he said: "Your concentration should be put more on the work, your work time on the computer says, you take a lot of breaks why is it so?" Sweety looked shocked at this questioning by Jeev.

Her eyes filled with tears, and she got up and ran to her cubicle. Jeev's approach was quite normal, but Sweety couldn't handle the slightest of comments from Jeev. She remained silent the entire day, without taking a break or talking to anyone, in spite of her newly made friends consoling her, she wept.

At that moment Jeev realized that Sweety was extremely sensitive and fragile at her emotions.

Jeev at the time of logout, called Sweety "Madam, it is my duty as your senior to guide you and give quality feedback, do not mistake me". Sweety was in no mood to listen to him. She started walking off, Jeev was feeling extremely uncomfortable having to deal with a child-like emotional girl. He ran to her and said "Okay, come I shall buy you chocolate ice cream". Sweety's eyes brightened up, she said "Sure sir, Okay".

It was probably after many many years Jeev went out with a person like this, and he felt extremely uncomfortable. They sat at the nearby cafe. Sweety spoke, "Sir, extremely sorry for being so sensitive, I want to say something to you, sir". "Tell me, madam," Jeev said. "Sir, I have no idea about your past, but I am madly in love with you sir, if you agree I want to marry you".

Jeev stood up shocked, in all that life, had he ever met a person who was so bold in her approach. Jeev didn't utter a single word and left the cafe. Walking down the road to his bike to head home. Jeev was suffering mentally, he wasn't open to a relationship, but did he have a liking for Sweety?

Sweety was not a normal person, she hadn't fallen in love ever in her life, Jeev was her first love. Jeev committed that he would live his entire life without any relationship approach. Here he is again in the cycle of people falling in love with him. Who is this Jeev? Who is this Sweety?

Jeev had no idea that Sweety had decided that she would spend the rest of her life with Jeev or not get married at all. Jeev here walked by and decided that it is impossible to agree to Sweety. Jeev had undergone a traumatic experience for a year, he did not come out of his home most of the days in the past 6 months, except at the workplace he never did anything. Jeev's behavior was extremely suspicious. Could looks cheat? could eyes cheat?

Sweety committed herself that she would be committed to Jeev till death, but Jeev had left.

SEVEN

Blood Sweat and Tears

3 months passed by, and hardly any conversation with Jeev, Sweety grew pale, it was Jeev's birthday.

Sweety had kept all her trainee money stored for celebrating Jeev's birthday. Her world was only Jeev now, it might find quite obsessive, but obsessive people do exist in the world.

Jeev usually does not come to the office on his birthday, since his childhood days Jeev had no interest in celebrating of his birthday nor he wanted to receive any wishes from anyone. Sweety waited for Jeev to arrive at the office and waited till 12 PM Jeev hadn't arrived and the manager said Jeev is on leave.

Sweety rang up Jeev, and Jeev wouldn't respond back to calls or messages. Jeev was finding Sweety's actions quite compulsive, yet she was an innocent girl who spent her entire thought process thinking about Jeev. Jeev finally responded to her call, Sweety said "Sir, please meet me today, I will never trouble you ever again"

Jeev agreed hesitantly and they both met near a shopping mart for the first time.

Sweety looked deep into Jeev's eyes, she had seen Jeev suffering from cold all the while, she had brought a sweater for Jeev, and she gifted it.

Jeev remained silent, Sweety asked," Sir, would you at least buy me something to eat, I have come all the way without having my food." Jeev's heart broke, Jeev wasn't a bad person but in terms of love and relationship, he was quite skeptical to get into any relationship. His past was hurting him.

Jeev received a letter from Sweety for his birthday, and they both went to the cafe. *Prakash came and stood nearby the cafe*, he stared at Sweety, but she didn't notice him. Prakash probably liked Jeev, but he wasn't sure, *Prakash has grown more of an observer and tried to be silent.*

Sweety on the other hand opened up, she said "Sir, I am extremely sorry to have brought you here, I wish you a very happy birthday!" I just wanted to wish you in person". It was late in the evening, the sun turned orange. Jeev thanked her for the wishes. Sweety had spent her entire salary savings to celebrate Jeev's birthday. She had ordered a cake, a bunch of small gifts to open and a precious letter, the letter that could break the heart!

Sweety had written a letter, she opened up the letter and gave it to Jeev, as he was reading the letter, he realized the letter wasn't written in blue color but by her blood. He threw the letter in shock.

He shouted, "You are a toxic person, I can't imagine someone doing this for me". Sweety stayed calm, and with her left hand bandaged she stood. In a moment's time, the entire childhood friends of Jeev came and surrounded him, Jeev's best friends, classmates and some office friends gathered at Jeev's birthday! What turned out to be a silent celebration has now turned into a birthday bash.

Jeev was in utter shock!

A small backdrop for Jeev's shock

Jeev had avoided all his friends, relatives, and close friends for a few years, he didn't believe in friendship or love relationships. He was now in a state of self-obsession. He enjoyed his own company. He didn't feel the need to be happy with people.

The research says, people who are happy, made relationships, shared, and cared for tend to live better in life, Sweety was one such person. But not Jeev.

This birthday bash changed Jeev as a person, he reconnected with a lot of his friends, and they rekindled the dead person in him. Jeev felt more alive after years!

Everyone left, except Sweety! She stood silent staring at Jeev. Jeev had really no choice but to surrender to the madness exhibited by Sweety! Without thinking twice, he ran towards Sweety and hugged her, Sweety's cheeks on his chest! It felt the warmest! It felt like the lost kid had reconnected to his mother, it felt at home!

Jeev had fallen in love with Sweety! It took blood, sweat, and Sweety's tears to fall in love! It was baptism by blood!

EIGHT

CASTLE OF LIES

For Jeev everything was new, there were plenty of reasons for Jeev to not get committed and now he s committed to one of the best human beings he could ask for! He was committed to the queen from hill station!

Jeev had a philosophy in life, he either gives his 201 percent in anything or nothing at all. Now he decided that he would give his everything to this relationship! It was indeed a tough decision to take, but he took the path, the path of the bloodshed may be.

Jeev for the next few months texted Sweety, and they saw each other, she carried lunch for him at times, she shared, he cared! That period was the golden period of their life.

Jeev suddenly stopped to receive or pick any of Sweety's calls, he would simply text her, and respond only in text, in spite of their meeting in the office every day, they being committed, Jeev although being committed in the relationship with Sweety, suddenly turned cold to her.

Sweety would literally beg Jeev to pick up the phone to speak to him, there was something that was bothering Jeev to pick up the call and speak. What was going through the mind of Jeev? The love story that began with blood and tears, might again lead to downfall.

Jeev believed in honesty at the cost of *white lies*, white lie is a process of lying to someone in order to protect them from being hurt or at the cost of saving them from immediate danger. Jeev's previous life experiences made him adjust his lifestyle for white lies.

Day by day slowly Jeev started avoiding Sweety, in messages he started expressing to her that he wishes to be her well-wisher and not true love. This baffled Sweety at times, she was the one who would never give up on him. She pursued him. Suddenly one evening! News channels alerted, due to the virus COVID- 19, there would be a countrywide lockdown that would be announced and Jeev's office announced work from home.

Sweety was disappointed because she couldn't meet her prince every day, but at the same time she was happy she could bombard Jeev with text messages every day. Jeev was in despair.

Slowly Jeev's messages to Sweety turned less, he started ignoring her messages, it was very hard for Sweety to undergo so much turmoil in her first love! She asked for this! They spent the entire pandemic by Jeev ignoring messages of Sweety. It was time for the office to reopen with 2 days of working. Offices resumed!

Jeev saw Sweety, the old Jeev that Sweety saw was changed, he looked different, extremely different, Jeev's face grew pale, he looked without energy, and his body language suggested that he was undergoing some kind of severe trauma or depression. But as soon as he saw her, he smiled. For a moment looking into their eyes of Sweety, Jeev regretted avoiding her! and he left.

NINE

HUG

Sweety grew anxious, adamant, and angered over the attitude of Jeev, she decided she would take control of her life. She texted Jeev, and she said I don't know I will be waiting for you at an address, we are meeting! she dropped the text and left for the address!

Jeev who hadn't spoken to Sweety in days now rushed to the address she sent, they met, and he saw her, Sweety in complete tears! She had no patience in waiting to convince him once again, that she wanted all his love. She hugged him, she hugged him in the tightest possible way, this wasn't the hug of love, this wasn't the hug of romance, this was the hug of hope!

Jeev's throat choked, he wasn't answering as to why he avoided her, Sweety was in no mood for reasons, she wanted to know why Jeev after getting committed was avoiding her.

Jeev answered, " Sweety, I don't think I am a suitable person who could, fit into your life, I have neither richness nor a future nor a good stable job to support you". He continued " My life is a series of disasters, nobody ever was happy staying in my life, being with me would definitely ruin your life". Saying so, he stopped. Sweety stood there hugging him, unaware of what the public would think, she was this girl, all that mattered to her was her life and her Jeev.

The problem with most of the Indian middle-class boys is they come from humble beginnings, they get a decent education, get into jobs, and start earning some amount of money, only to realize that the money they are earning is less compared to the responsibilities they have. Adding to the responsibilities are the parent's health issues, siblings' marriages, and being stuck with personal goals and ambitions. Stuck in this cycle, falling in love is definitely an additional responsibility. Apart from this, something else was bothering Jeev. Jeev never shared his pain or suffering with anyone.

He took Sweety's face in his palms, looked into her eyes deeply, kissed her forehead, kissed her eyes, and hugged her in his arms, and promised to be with her! Sweety felt warmth, the warmth that she longed for years. Jeev took Sweety into his bike and dropped her home, Sweety wouldn't leave his hands, she looked back many times, he got down from the vehicle, and she came back running, he held her tight, he hugged her like it was the last time they hugged, Sweety showered loads of kisses, she wouldn't leave, Jeev asked, do you love me, baby? She said "NO" and she hugged him back, Jeev kissed her both eyes and sent her back. Prakash saw her, he observed it, and he smiled!

Jeev left!

TEN
DHARMA

Jeev took a leave from his office, and so did Sweety, Jeev for some reason didn't believe that they both could live together, but he promised himself that till the day they both are together, he would do everything possible for Sweety in the capacity of a husband. He believed that taking care of her and her happiness is Dharma. Dharma according to Jeev was being right for that person, he was ready to go against the entire system to protect her.

He took her out to a nearby meditation place, Jeev believed Sweety should explore the city and kept her happy. Jeev also believed in long-term happiness rather than short-term fun in spending time in malls and shopping places is useless.

Sweety wanted to get married to Jeev, she expressed her willingness to get married. She said " Jeev please get married to me" and she has no time left to get married, so Sweety did sometimes pressurize Jeev.

Sweety can get married but it was a marriage between two different castes, it was a marriage between two different languages, and Sweety put up a condition to the marriage, that post the marriage they would want to settle down abroad, stating the reason that their relatives arent kind enough people and she wants to spend the rest of her life, in peace.

Prakaash, Sweety's brother had requested Sweety that she should settle in abroad and it was his dream.

For Jeev who comes from a very lower middle-class background paying his home rent and meeting his expenses was a big deal, imagining abroad was a far-fetched dream. But for Sweety and her happiness he had to do it.

If middle-class boy decides he wants to move mountains for his love, he shall move!

Jeev spoke " Sweety, I believe in family, supporting the family, I can get married to you, but the condition of being abroad was definitely not happening". Sweety looking at his response broke, she cried loud, deep inside they both knew that their relationship wouldn't last long, Jeev had just seen a Tamil movie, relating to the chief minister of Tamil Nadu who fell in love with a lady but couldn't marry her, but with dearness, he called her Ammu!

Jeev called Sweety "Ammu" for the first time! Sweety felt better, she called him back "Ammu"! It felt the best, probably Ammu is a word that is kept for the nearest and dearest ones who couldn't stay in one's life! From then on Jeev called her "AMMU, the queen who brought love from hill station!

Jeev believed giving her false hopes of marriage wasn't his Dharma! He also believed loving someone and marrying someone else was not also the Dharma, Sweety believed loving and living for Jeev was her only Dharma!

ELEVEN

Promise to Build Castle of Lies

Jeev came back running that night, he gave himself a promise, he said " I would do everything to keep her happy, Everything in this world!" he shouted, he shouted loud. This might come at a cost, the cost probably that Jeev wasn't even aware of or he was aware!

The next day, Jeev came with his car, that car that he had purchased a few years back, it was a second-hand car, and he wanted to meet Sweety every time with this car of his. It was an old dark green Santro car, he had but the car was strong and tough like Jeev.

Sweety called Jeev " Where are you", Jeev said he was in Chennai, the fast process for applying for Visa was in Chennai, and the Visa was for applying for a job in the UK. Sweety was shocked, what she didn't expect from Jeev was now happening, Jeev had applied to many jobs and had given interviews online and had gotten a job in the UK. It was pending approval in Chennai, every year there are thousands of job aspirants who leave the country in the hope of better life, and better money, here was our hero who was leaving for abroad for the purpose of his love!

Just middle-class things!

Sweety cried with joy. Her future looked strong, Jeev was doing the impossible. In a day or two Jeev returned back from Chennai, and he met Sweety for their regular dose of love.

TWELVE

Daana Veera Shoora Karna

One fine afternoon, both Ammu couples, had visited the shopping street, Jeev hadn't gifted anything to Sweety all the while, Sweety was a traditional Indian girl who loved sarees. It was time for Jeev to buy her a saree.

Jeev bought the best of the saree for Sweety, they loved it, and they lived like there was no tomorrow! Sweety's eyes brightened not because he bought her a saree, it was a very emotional connection between them. Soon enough she got calls from her mother, her mother wanted her to be home soon. Jeev dropped her back. Before leaving Sweety expressed that soon she would want to meet his parents!

Jeev came back home and sat at his desk, he wanted to have a cup of coffee, he went to the kitchen, prepared, and drank the hot coffee with extra sugar.

He lied down on his bed, it was early evening, and his eyes filled with tears! He was waiting for the Visa approval and plans to clear off his loans, and avail of a new loan to travel abroad with his Ammu!

Jeev received continuous calls from some unknown numbers, which he ignored, he was scared at times, what were these calls? Jeev paid the rent, and other bills pending, and went to the hospital only to see his ailing sister at the hospital who was suffering from severe mental abnormalities, Jeev kept this a secret, he had to spend one-fourth of his salary on her treatment. His sister was counting her days! Jeev made the necessary payments and left for the day.

THIRTEEN

THE BAD SIDE TO A GOOD CAUSE

Jeev was disappointed when he learnt that the visa was rejected! Jeev grew more impatient, he threw his tantrums at Sweety, just like any toxic relationship, he too did turn this beautiful relationship into a toxic one.

Not that Jeev wasn't aware of his toxic behaviour but he still expressed his discontentment over the innocent Sweety.

Sweety had a lot of brothers apart from Prakaash, her juniors from school, college, and other places were still in touch. This irritated Jeev a lot, every time he would see her engaged in the phone with one of her friends or one of her brothers.

Although Sweety knew her limitations, Jeev insisted on quitting the entire circle of friends. Sweety made new friends with her trainees in the office, Sweety's best friend was Diksha. Jeev's insecurity forced her to even maintain distance from her own friends. Jeev who was the best man she could ask for in life had turned into an ultra-possessive, doubting monstrous creature. It reached a stage where most of the trainees saw Sweety's face losing interest in work, she walked alone and hardly saw her on the phone.

What boys fail to understand in a girl is, her world no matter what the world says is a very limited place. Her circle and her world is small. Friends, phones and social media are the only source of entertainment and relaxation she has compared to the adventurous and hyper active men's habits. She since her childhood has been restricted to do anything and everything, from going out to parties, outings, trips and night outs, everything is restricted. She comes to the relationship with a small glimmer of hope that she could breathe a bit more freely and not feel restricted in the space.

Yet here was Ammu, who got caught at the wrong side of a right man! There were continuous quarrels, every time Jeev mentioned let's break up! Sweety no matter what wasn't ready to quit the relationship. Sweety had seen something in the eyes of Jeev, she felt Jeev couldn't do this to her.

Sweety met Jeev after office hours, she wanted to rekindle the love that was turning toxic, she held the palms of Jeev and reminded him about the kind of person he was! Jeev held Sweety after a long time in his palms, he took her near and without hesitation kissed her lips! It was the first time they grew intimate in their relationship. Could intimacy save the relationship? Soon Sweety kept her head on Jeev's chest and she cried, Jeev although felt extremely regretful at his behaviour, something was bothering him. He took Sweety by his arms, she slept there for some time, there was a silence, the silence was peaceful.

Prakaash from far saw everything, the only thing that Prakaash did not appreciate was the tears from Sweety's eyes and the pain that Jeev gave. Yet, Prakaash was in favour of Jeev. Maybe they both were brothers in some life! Consoling Sweety Jeev left. so did Prakaash.

Was Jeev intentional in doing these acts? was he really cruel? Something was not right?

FOURTEEN
LIE TILL YOU DIE

One fine evening, Jeev received a call from Sweety. She had found a bunch of facts about Jeev that he had kept as secret, Jeev had not disclosed his proper salary to Sweety, and he had not given proper information about his family too.

Sweety grew suspicious, she changed as a person slowly, Sweety suffered from chronic pain from her varicose nerve. She had breathing problems sometimes, but she kept this hidden from Jeev. Due to the continuous toxicity that Jeev exhibited, Ammu had grown into deep sadness. It sometimes did feel for Ammu that she should move away from this relationship. She opened the photos of Jeev and she could see his smile and his deep eyes and she convinced herself that she would stay till the end of the relationship!

Sweety found out that Jeev was working two jobs a day, was not taking care of his health, and was also burdening himself with too much work, Jeev did sometimes say the white lie in order to protect the relationship.

Jeev lied about the location he visited, he lied about the food that he ate, he lied about the friends circle he had, some lies casual, some lies serious but all to protect Ammu's smile! Why did Jeev as a person get himself changed? From a more dependent person and loving caring gentleman to a hopeless human who couldn't take care of his little one? Is it fair to construct a relationship with the castle of white lies?

FIFTEEN

Doors Closed

It was a fine morning, Jeev had promised to visit Ammu's house to talk about their marriage, and Jeev had also promised that he would visit Ammu's house with his mother.

Ammu the night before was extremely excited because Jeev had also promised Ammu that he would speak to their parents in their local language Tamil and he would learn the entire language. Ammu's mother who normally would not agree to the marriage felt a strong negative vibe toward Jeev. She did not want to disappoint her daughter. She agreed to meet Jeev.

They made arrangements, she brought sweets, she brought all the necessary items to welcome the love of her life, in spite of the amount of pain she underwent. A part of her felt alive and excited, she finally felt that she would live her life with Jeev!

It was morning 10, the time that Jeev had promised that he would turn up. It turned 10 and Ammu waiting for Jeev's and his mother's arrival. The clock turned 11, and there are no signs of any visitors, the clock ticked 12 and Ammu's parents grew furious about Jeev's attitude, although Ammu's dad was still hoping that the boy isn't a bad person. Ammu's mother did not appreciate the effort, it was 2 PM, Ammu and her parents decided to not to stay at home and waste a Sunday. They headed out. Where was Jeev? Is Jeev a cheater?

Ammu called Jeev many times, but the phone was not reachable or switched off, Was the door to Ammu's heart and Ammu's home closed?

Where did Jeev leave?

SIXTEEN

HAPPY ENDING

Ammu literally left speaking to Jeev post that day, she did not bother to contact him back, although she underwent a tremendous amount of pressure without Jeev, his care, his love, his tantrums. She missed him every second! She breathed Jeev literally every second of her life. But the disappointment he caused couldn't be forgotten.

A few days passed by, and although Ammu had the urge to message Jeev, every lie, his behavior, and his attitude reminded her of the pain, yet she kept quiet.

Ammu one evening received a call from Darshi, Jeev's best friend, he said "Akka Jeev wants to speak to you immediately, please start immediately and come to his home near Kashinagar. Ammu said no she is not interested to talk or meeting Jeev anymore. Darshi's voice seemed a bit scary, his voice was a bit serious, Ammu the sensitive person she is towards Jeev started, and a part of her hope came alive.

She reached Jeev's place, she went inside Jeev's home, she had visited the home sometimes back but hadn't been familiar with family or home intensely. Darshi stood at the door, and welcomed Ammu without a proper smile.

Jeev is sitting inside, he might be a bit angry with you Akka, don't feel bad. He wants you to listen to this recording before you talk to him, or else you might fight again with him! Jeev also has decided to come to Kodaikanal after this meeting, please take him to Akka, saying this Darshi Left!

SEVENTEEN
The Record

Ammu played the recording on Jeev's phone "Ammu, I love you so much da! I know you are angry with me paapa, you are my world da. You might feel that I have cheated you, I have betrayed you, I have treated you badly at times, I have also insisted that you leave me and lead your life happily, but the mad love, you are! you never left me. Thanks for all the love you gave me paapa, these few days of love that we spent together are the best days of my life.

We did not care about society, we did not care about the office, and we loved like there is no tomorrow, if I could say my love was 1 percent, your contribution to our love was 99 percent! Ammu, I really love you so much, I want to spend the rest of my life with you da! But..

Ammu these facts might break your heart but before we meet I want to confess these facts to you, Ammu firstly, Ammu I am a poor boy from an extremely lower middle-class background, I do not earn a salary of a lakh plus as I have lied you, I earn much lesser amount than I said. Forgive me da..

Ammu I am not having any kind of family da, I lost my own parents even before I was born and even before I opened my eyes. I was an adopted son of my parents, they adopted me as their only daughter suffered from mental abnormalities. Forgive me da..

Ammu I did not grow up in a regular school or college background, all my life I spent working in menial jobs. I worked as a delivery boy, as a cashier as a call center worker as a maid, and as a driver in many private car firms. When you said abroad I really didn't cheat you, Ammu. I needed your love and could definitely not fulfill your wish of taking you abroad. Forgive me, Ammu..

Ammu my ex left me not because I did not take care of her, but because, I was poor and did not have the stability to take care of her post-marriage. Ammu all the gifts, sarees and other things iI purchased for us was out of a credit bill. Ammu I had to donate my blood at a private hospital to pay back the credit card bill sometimes! (Crying sound in the background) Ammu, I don't mean that I sacrificed everything for your happiness, Every boy of my age has dreams to take care of his girl in the best possible way and treat her like his queen. I tried my best to take care of you Ammu! Forgive me for lying Ammu..

Ammu I don't have my both parents alive to bring them to your home and seek your alliance da. I am really sorry paapa, Neither I have the monetary strength to provide for you nor the physical energy to take care of you. Forgive me, Ammu..

Ammu I had built the Castle of Lies to keep you happy paapa. But now I want to tell you why I hurt you, why I gave you pain, why did I always say let's break up, and why did I ignore you?

Ammu come inside my room while you are listening to this record., Ammu walked inside Jeev's room.

Jeev spoke (in the record) "Ammu I suffer from ***Multiple Sclerosis,*** **Take a deep breath Ammu.Ammu this is a autoimmune disease that affects the part of the brain and spinal cord. Ammu I was identified with this disease a year back we met. Ammu this disease is related to Central Nervous System. This disease destroys the vital parts of the body. I had severe hearing loss, and the eyesight had been reduced by more than 50 percentage. Ammu it causes anxiety and other health disorders and finally it shrinks the brain and causes a fatal death. Ammu my last wish is to visit Kodaikanal with you paapa..**

Ammu forgive me da! I am sitting in front of the vase that you are seeing, safely and in warmth! Yes Ammu I left this world. Yes

Ammu I left without saying you goodbye! Ammu, I need a promise that you would stay happily married and lead a life without me. I take this promise from you! Ammu remember I love you so much. I did not cheat you Ammu I wanted your love but I wanted your happiness too. Ammu I shall miss you! Yours Jeev!

Ammu fell in tears and in shock!

EIGHTEEN

JEEV VISITS KODAIKANAL

After a few days, Ammu carried the Ashes of Jeev and carried it to Kodaikanal. Ammu the queen from hill station carried her love back home! She missed Jeev more than hell and heaven. She carried his ashes in the vase and hugged him tight. It reminded her of the day when Jeev slept on her lap, it reminded her of the day when Jeev asked "Will you take me to Kodai? Pinky promise".

Ammu's brother was Prakaash, Ammu's brother Prakaash was dead a few years back before she came to Bengaluru. The presence of Prakaash was a mere illusion that Ammu always had about her brother staying near her to protect her. Poor Ammu fought hard to protect her love.

The Queen after a few years left for abroad, it has been many years since Jeev passed, and Ammu still lives in the memory of Jeev. Although Ammu is married and leading her life, yet her soul still yearns for Jeev.

A story by Jayanth Kashyap

Request

If you did like my novel AMMU, I humbly request you to please post your reviews on Amazon, Flipkart, and your social media handles, you can even tag my works and exhibit your appreciation by tagging us on Instagram @ Jayanthsacademy page.

In order to shower more love and support you can send me your honest review video byte of 1 minute each that shall be shared on my Instagram handle!

For direct feedback or any issue contact me @jayanthacademy@gmail.com

About The Author

Jayanth Kashyap is a writer and a YouTuber, he runs a youtube page called "Jayanth's Academy, and an Instagram page that promotes all his works.

Assistant professor by profession, yet his love for emotions and literature has made him pursue a career in writing. Now that I have taken my writing as a serious profession, I would promise to provide a minimum of one book every 4 months.

You can also read my other books on Amazon, Flipkart, and Notion press

1. 8 Chapters before you give up
2. Tell me the Reason Why you Left
3. Biography of a Con Artist

Do subscribe to my Youtube Channel to be continuously engaged in content that is abstract to the real world. ***Subscribe @ Jayanth's Academy***

9 798890 266279

Printed by Libri Plureos GmbH in Hamburg,
Germany